P9-BJQ-863

TOWER of TREASURE

THREE THIEVES · BOOK ONE

For Miles and Mason
Here, at long last, is the "story with a castle in it" that you asked for.

Kids Can Press acknowledges the financial support of the Government of Ontario, through the Ontario Media Development Corporation's Ontario Book Initiative; the Ontario Arts Council; the Canada Council for the Arts; and the Government of Canada, through the BPIDP, for our publishing activity.

Published in Canada by	Published in the U.S. by
Kids Can Press Ltd.	Kids Can Press Ltd.
25 Dockside Drive	2250 Military Road
Toronto, ON M5A 0B5	Tonawanda, NY 14150

www.kidscanpress.com

Pages lettered with Blambot comic fonts.

Edited by Karen Li
Designed by Kathleen Gray and Scott Chantler

The hardcover edition of this book is smyth sewn casebound.
The paperback edition of this book is limp sewn with a drawn-on cover.
Manufactured in Tsuen Wan, NT, in 6/2011 by WKT Company

CM 10 0 9 8 7 6 5 4 3 2
CM PA 10 0 9 8 7 6 5 4 3 2

Library and Archives Canada Cataloguing in Publication

Chantler, Scott
    Tower of treasure / Scott Chantler.

ISBN 978-1-55453-414-2 (bound). ISBN 978-1-55453-415-9 (pbk.)

I. Title. II. Series: Chantler, Scott. Three thieves.

PS8605.H3566T69 2010   j741.5'971   C2009-901521-8

Kids Can Press is a *Corus*™ Entertainment company

TOWER of TREASURE

THREE THIEVES · BOOK ONE

Scott Chantler

Kids Can Press

ACT ONE
TIGHTROPE

GOD'S TEETH! LOOK AT ALL THE PEOPLE.

IT'S EVEN MORE CROWDED THAN FLAGFORD AND LOGGERHEAD.

FORGET THE *PEOPLE*...THINK OF ALL THE *MONEY!*

I DUNNO, TOPPER...THEY ACTUALLY LOOK PRETTY *POOR.*

NOT DOWN HERE, YOU PUTTOCK.

UP *THERE.*

ALL THE QUEEN'S WEALTH. RIGHT THERE IN THAT TOWER.

THEY SAY HER TREASURY HOLDS MORE GOLD THAN A DRAGON'S DEN.

BUT IF I *DID*, IT'D BE A GREAT WAY TO SOLIDIFY MY REPUTATION AS—

—AS "THE GREATEST THIEF IN NORTH HUNTINGTON"?

PFFT. THE ONLY PERSON I'VE EVER HEARD SAY THAT IS *YOU.*

PEOPLE SAY IT ALL THE TIME!

WHAT PEOPLE?

LOTS OF PEOPLE.

AND JUST HOW WOULD *YOU* KNOW WHERE THE QUEEN'S TREASURY IS, ANYWAY?

MAYBE— JUST MAYBE— I HAVE A *MAP OF THE PALACE.*

I'M SURE I'LL FEEL SORRY FOR ASKING, BUT WHERE'D YOU GET IT?

I BOUGHT IT YEARS AGO FROM A COOK WHO WORKED IN THE PALACE KITCHEN.

OKAY. SO HOW WOULD THE *COOK* KNOW WHERE THE TREASURY IS?

HE WOULDN'T. BUT HIS BROTHER KNEW A GUY WHO CARRIED SOME GOLD UP THERE ONCE.

"HIS *BROTHER* KNEW A *GUY*"...?

I WAS RIGHT...I'M SORRY I ASKED.

11

YOU'RE GONNA BE EVEN SORRIER WHEN *WE'RE* RICH AND *YOU'RE* NOT.

HERE WE ARE, LAGGARDS!

IT'S TOO BAD, REALLY. WE COULD HAVE USED YOUR SKILLS FOR THIS JOB.

"WE"?

WHO'S "WE"?

WHAT'RE WE TALKIN' ABOUT?

ROBBIN' THE TREASURY?

GAH!

NO ONE IS ROBBING THE TREASURY!

13

NOT MUCH OF AN AUDIENCE FOR SUCH A LARGE CITY...

DO YOU SEE HIM, DEAR?

WHICH ONE?

WELL...EITHER OF THEM, I GUESS.

ONLY WHEN I *CLOSE* MY EYES.

WHERE IS THE BOY?

WHERE ARE YOU HIDING HIM, WOMAN? I WON'T ASK AGAIN.

I WON'T GIVE UP MY SON.

NOT TO YOU.

THEN MAYBE HE'LL GIVE *HIMSELF* UP.

BURN THE HOUSE.

SIR?

THAT'S AN *ORDER*, MEN.

BURN IT.

19

SIGH.

WAIT...

HEY!

WAIT!

HEY!

WHAT ARE YOU—?

OOOF!

I'M *SORRY*, HUGO.

"SORRY" ISN'T GONNA *FEED* US TONIGHT, YOU LITTLE BEAST.

WHAT ABOUT YOU? DID *YOU* GET ANYTHING?

HOW *COULD* I?

THIS IS YOUR FAULT, GIRL!

PLEASE, HUGO! DON'T DROP MY ACT!

I HAVE TO KEEP LOOKING FOR—

I'M NOT GONNA DROP YOUR ACT.

BUT YOU'D BETTER COME UP WITH A WAY TO FEED US TONIGHT, OR *I'LL WRING YOUR SCRAWNY NECK!*

HUGO, YOU *KNOW* I HATE STEALING...

WELL, YOU KNOW WHAT *I* HATE?

GOING HUNGRY!

HEH. *THAT* MUCH IS OBVIOUS.

ULP.

DON'T EVEN *THINK* ABOUT COMING BACK HERE, DESSA...

...NOT UNTIL YOU'VE FOUND US *FOOD*, OR THE MONEY TO *BUY* SOME!

NOW RUN ALONG, LITTLE GIRL.

RUN ALONG.

FISK?

OH...HI, DESSA!

IS THIS REALLY WHAT IT'S COME TO, FISK? *BEGGING?*

BECAUSE I DON'T THINK YOU'RE GOING TO DO VERY WELL. THIS ENTIRE CITY SEEMS TO BE BROKE.

HUH?

OH, NO...I'M JUST WAITING FOR TOPPER.

OKAY.

SO WHERE IS HE?

UP THERE.

OH, RIGHT.

THE BIG *TREASURY HEIST.*

LISTEN, BIG GUY, I DON'T REALLY KNOW HOW TO TELL YOU THIS...

...BUT I THINK TOPPER'S PUTTING ONE OVER ON YOU. HE'S PROBABLY BACK AT THE WAGON RIGHT NOW, LAUGHING THE POINTS OFF HIS EARS.

THINK ABOUT IT. I MEAN, HOW WOULD HE EVEN GET UP THERE?

HE CRAWLED IN THROUGH THE DRAIN.

THE *DRAIN?!*

HA!

NOW I'VE HEARD EVERYTHING!

WHY WOULD A *TREASURY* HAVE A *DRAINAGE SYSTEM?*

WELL, OKAY...

BUT THIS IS TOO SMALL FOR ANYONE BUT —

LAST CHANCE, DESSA.

YOU WANNA HELP US OR NOT?

ACT TWO
TRAPS

I'M SO HUNGRY!

BAH! SCAVENGING DOG!

AWAY FROM THE PALACE BEFORE WE CLAP YOU IN IRONS!

PLEASE, GUARDSMAN!

JUST A CRUST OF BREAD?

WHAT'S THE PROBLEM HERE, MEN?

CAPTAIN DRAKE!

N-NOTHING, SIR.

I-I BARELY REMEMBER RODERICK, SIR.

ME NEITHER. I WAS ONLY A BOY WHEN HE WAS ON THE THRONE.

DON'T LET ME KEEP YOU, MEN.

BACK TO YOUR PATROL.

YES, SIR.

THANK YOU, SIR.

I CAN'T BELIEVE WE'RE DOING THIS! WHAT IF WE GET CAUGHT?

I'M NOT PLANNING ON GETTING CAUGHT.

OH, GOOD. YOU MEAN UNLIKE THE OTHER ONES WHO *DO?*

LISTEN, IF YOU'D RATHER CLIMB BACK DOWN AND WANDER THE STREETS LOOKING FOR FOOD, I'M SURE FISK WOULD BE HAPPY TO LOWER THE ROPE.

NOW STOP COMPLAINING AND WATCH OUT FOR BOOBY TRAPS.

"BOOBY TRAPS"? THE QUEEN'S TREASURY IS *BOOBY-TRAPPED?*

WOULDN'T *YOURS* BE?

GOOD POINT.

SO, WHAT ARE THE TRAPS? AND WHERE ARE THEY?

YOUR MAP DOESN'T *SAY?*

UGH.

THE COOK'S BROTHER'S FRIEND NEVER ACTUALLY SET FOOT IN THIS TOWER, DID HE?

SURE HE DID!

THE TRAPS WERE *JUST DISARMED* THEN, SO THEY COULD BRING THE GOLD UP! HOW WOULD *HE* KNOW WHAT THEY ARE?

MAKES SENSE...I GUESS.

SO, WHAT ARE WE LOOKING FOR? TRIP WIRES? FALSE FLOORS?

TAP TAP

...NOTHING THAT SOPHISTICATED, I DON'T THINK.

PROBABLY MORE LIKE—

Click!

THUNK

39

OOOF!

OKAY.

NOW WHAT?

I'VE GOT AN IDEA.

THAT'S WHAT I WAS AFRAID OF.

AND I DON'T LIKE THE LOOK OF THOSE GARGOYLES.

GIMME THAT TORCH.

TAP

WHOOOOSH

SO, WHAT DO WE DO NOW?

THERE MUST BE A WAY TO DISARM IT.

THERE IS...

...THERE.

OKAY.

BUT HOW DO WE *GET* TO IT?

LIKE *THIS!*

GOD'S TEETH!

OPEN THAT DOOR!

SIR?

OPEN IT!

THERE'S SOMEONE IN THE TOWER.

THE QUEEN MIGHT AS WELL HAVE *BLIND MEN* GUARD THIS DOOR.

THERE MUST BE SOME MISTAKE, SIR.

WE HAVEN'T LET ANYONE P—

SUMMON AS MANY OTHER GUARDS AS YOU CAN. I WANT EVERY AVAILABLE MAN. DO IT QUICKLY.

AND YOU...

...GO FIND *MAARTEN GREYFALCON.*

IT'LL BE *LOCKED*, OF COURSE.

OF COURSE.

BUT I THINK THE SOLUTION TO *THIS* ONE IS OBVIOUS.

FISK?

BAM

SUBTLE.

THOUGH YOU'D THINK "THE GREATEST THIEF IN NORTH HUNTINGTON" COULD HAVE JUST *PICKED THE LOCK.*

THIS IS MORE MY STYLE.

YOU COMIN', OR WHAT?

WOOO-HOOO!

WE'RE RICH! RICH, I TELLS YA!

I CAN'T BELIEVE IT...

...QUEEN MAGDA HAS ALL THIS JUST *SITTING* HERE, WHILE HER PEOPLE ARE DOWN THERE GOING HUNGRY.

WELL, NO MORE GOING HUNGRY FOR *US!*

AND NO MORE PERFORMING LIKE MONKEYS FOR THAT FAT CANKER-BLOSSOM AND HIS THIRD-RATE SIDESHOW, EITHER!

WE'RE RICH!

I DUNNO.

THIS WAS TOO EASY.

"EASY?!"

YOU'VE FORGOTTEN THE *STAIRS?* THE *FIRE-BREATHING HALLWAY?*

IF *I* WERE SETTING TRAPS HERE, I'D WAIT UNTIL THE MOMENT THE ROBBERS FELT LIKE THEY'D SUCCEEDED, THEN I'D HIT THEM WITH...

ANOTHER LEVER?

YEP.

JUST LIKE THE ONE IN THE HALL.

SO LET'S *PULL* IT!

IT'LL DISARM WHATEVER TRAP IS IN HERE, THEN WE CAN BEAT IT WITH THE GOLD!

NO!

THINK, TOPPER!

WHOEVER PLANNED THESE TRAPS WAS COUNTING ON US HAVING USED THE LEVER OUTSIDE TO DISARM THE TRAP IN THE HALL...

...SO HE PUT THIS ONE HERE, HOPING WE'D PULL *IT,* TOO. IT PROBABLY *SPRINGS* THE TRAP!

OKAY, THEN. SO WE *WON'T* PULL THE LEVER! WHATEVER MAKES YOU HAPPY!

NOW START FILLING A SACK, AND LET'S GET OUTTA HERE...

55

HA!

WE'RE ALIVE!

UH... TOPPER?

NOT ONLY THAT, BUT ALL THE GOLD IS STILL HERE WITH US!

HOW OLD ARE YOU, GIRL?

I DON'T KNOW. I LOST COUNT ALONG THE WAY.

FOURTEEN, MAYBE.

HM. AND WHERE ARE YOUR MOTHER AND FATHER?

I DON'T HAVE A FATHER.

THEN WHERE IS YOUR MOTHER?

LISTEN, CAPTAIN ONE-EYE! *NOBODY* GOT ROBBED! WE WERE JUST—

ACK!

BUMP

YOU WERE *SAYING...?*

WHAT HAVE WE HERE, CAPTAIN?

THREE THIEVES, MASTER GREYFALCON. RESOURCEFUL ONES, TOO.

THEY MADE IT ALL THE WAY INTO THE TREASURE CHAMBER, BEFORE GETTING CAUGHT IN YOUR—

YOU.

68

WHERE'S MY BROTHER, YOU DEVIL?

DON'T PRETEND YOU DON'T KNOW WHAT I'M TALKING ABOUT, MURDERER!

WHAT DID YOU DO WITH HIM?!

YOUR... BROTHER?

OH.

73

74

ACT THREE
THE CHAMBERLAIN'S SECRET

I'M SORRY I HAVE TO DO THIS.

BUT IF I DON'T, YOUR LARGE FRIEND HERE WILL SIMPLY TEAR DOWN THE DOOR.

AND WE CAN'T HAVE ANY OF *THAT.*

SO YOU'RE *REALLY* GOING TO LET THEM HANG US?

IT'S JUST...THE WAY YOU STOOD UP TO THE CHAMBERLAIN, I THOUGHT—

I SERVE THE THRONE, NOT MAARTEN GREYFALCON.

IF THE QUEEN SAYS YOU HANG, THEN YOU HANG.

JUST LIKE THAT, HUH?

SHE SAYS, "JUMP," YOU ASK "HOW HIGH?"

I THOUGHT YOU WERE A KNIGHT, NOT SOME HALF-PENNY STRUMPET!

MIND YOUR TONGUE WITH ME, NORKER.

IT'S ON MY ACCOUNT THAT YOU STILL DRAW BREATH AT ALL.

I'LL RETURN IN THE MORNING TO SEE THE QUEEN'S SENTENCE CARRIED OUT.

YOU'VE BEEN GIVEN A FEW MORE HOURS TO LIVE. DON'T WASTE THEM WITH FURTHER FOOLISHNESS, OR DESPERATE THOUGHTS OF ESCAPE.

GIVEN YOUR CIRCUMSTANCES, I SUGGEST YOU USE THEM TO BEG FOR MERCY FROM WHICHEVER GODS YOU PRAY TO.

...SO THEN THE JESTER ASKS THE PEASANT, "ARE YOU A HORSE'S *HOOF?*" AND THE PEASANT SAYS, "NO."

THEN THE JESTER ASKS, "ARE YOU A HORSE'S *HEAD?*" AND THE PEASANT SAYS "NO" AGAIN.

HEH HEH.

"IN THAT CASE," THE JESTER SAYS, "YOU MUST BE A HORSE'S—"

KLUNK!

I TAKE BACK ALL THE BAD THINGS I EVER SAID ABOUT YOU, TOPPER.

YOU REALLY *MIGHT* BE THE BEST THIEF AROUND. THAT LIFT YOU PULLED ON THE CAPTAIN WAS SMOOTH AS SILK.

GLAD YOU'RE HAPPY. NOW LET'S FIND A WAY OUT OF HERE.

YOU'VE STILL GOT YOUR *MAP?*

YEAH, I—

GIMME THAT.

YOU THINK I CAN'T FIND US A WAY OUT?

I'M NOT LOOKING FOR A WAY OUT. I'M LOOKING FOR THE CHAMBERLAIN'S QUARTERS.

WHAT?!

DESSA, THAT'S SO CRAZY EVEN I WOULDN'T TRY IT!

THERE.

YOU HEARD WHAT CAPTAIN UGLY SAID! WE'RE LUCKY TO BE ALIVE!

WE NEED TO DISAPPEAR—NOW —BEFORE THAT LUCK FINALLY RUNS OUT!

HE'S RIGHT, DESSA.

I KNOW HE IS.

BUT DID YOU SEE THE WAY THE QUEEN LOOKED AT GREYFALCON? HE'S INVOLVED IN SOMETHING EVEN *SHE* DIDN'T KNOW ABOUT.

AND IT INVOLVES MY BROTHER, SOMEHOW.

YOU TWO NEED TO ESCAPE, AND I HOPE YOU CAN.

BUT I'M NOT LEAVING UNTIL I FIND OUT WHAT'S GOING ON.

EVEN IF I HAVE TO *DIE* TRYING!

LONG NIGHT, CAPTAIN?

YOU HAVE NO IDEA.

WELL, IT'LL BE OVER SOON ENOUGH.

THE GALLOWS HERE WILL BE READY BY SUNRISE.

GOD'S TEETH!

WHY ARE YOU SNEAKING AWAY IN THE MIDDLE OF THE—?

SEARCH THE PALACE!

THE PRISONERS HAVE ESCAPED!

GREYFALCON!

THE THIEVES HAVE ESCAPED! THEY—!

KLUNK

91

SUN'S NEARLY UP.

I'LL GO TELL CAPTAIN DRAKE WE'RE READY FOR THE PRISONERS N—

WHAT IN THE AVATAR'S BEARD IS *THAT?!*

SHE'S HEADED FOR THE WEST GATE.

CHUK

RUMBLE RUMBLE RU—

HA!

"FIRST, YOU WAKE ME IN THE MIDDLE OF THE NIGHT TO SETTLE A SENSELESS DISPUTE BETWEEN YOURSELF AND MAARTEN GREYFALCON..."

"...THEN YOU ALLOW THREE PRISONERS TO ESCAPE BY LETTING A TWO-BIT PICKPOCKET GET THE BETTER OF YOU..."

"...AND NOW YOU TELL ME THAT THE ROYAL CHAMBERLAIN IS NOWHERE TO BE FOUND!"

OUTRAGEOUS!

MY FATHER THOUGHT YOU THE GREATEST OF ALL HIS KNIGHTS, CAPTAIN DRAKE. AS DO I. YOUR LOYALTY TO ME, AND TO HIM, HAS BEEN EXEMPLARY.

BUT YOU'VE FOULED THIS UP MOST HORRIBLY.

TO ALLOW US TO BE MADE FOOLS OF, AND BY A MERE *GIRL!*

WITH ALL DUE RESPECT, YOUR MAJESTY, THIS IS NO MERE GIRL. THE MEN SAY SHE MOVES LIKE A CAT. AND SEEMS TO HAVE AS MANY LIVES.

SHE'S NOT SOME SUPERNATURAL CREATURE, CAPTAIN. SHE IS FLESH AND BLOOD.

AND I WANT TO KNOW WHAT SHE'S DONE WITH GREYFALCON.

ASSEMBLE MY DRAGONS.

ALL OF THEM, MADAM?

ALL OF THEM.

"YOU'LL RIDE OUT IMMEDIATELY. AT FULL STRENGTH."

"YOU'LL SCOUR THE WHOLE KINGDOM, IF YOU NEED TO. CHASE THEM TO WHERE THE EARTH MEETS THE SKY, IF THAT'S WHAT'S REQUIRED."

"BUT YOU'LL NOT RETURN UNLESS IT'S WITH THE HEADS OF THESE THREE THIEVES."

CLOP CLOP

CLOP
CLOP
CLOP

CLOP
CLOP

I'M GOING *WEST*.

SAME AS GREYFALCON.

I FOUND THIS IN HIS CHAMBER. IT'S SOME KIND OF NOTEBOOK.

IT'S GOT PLANS FOR ALL SORTS OF STRANGE CONTRAPTIONS...

...LIKE THAT FLYING MACHINE THERE.

MAYBE IT'S GOT *OTHER* SECRETS IN IT, TOO.

DARKER SECRETS.

BUT UNTIL I FIND OUT, I'M GOING TO STAY ON HIS TRAIL.

LIKE A BLOODHOUND.

I HAD A HORSE AND SENT IT SOUTH, TO THROW OFF WHOEVER COMES AFTER US.

SO WHEREVER YOU GO, DON'T GO *THAT* WAY.

WELL, WE WERE THINKIN' OF GOIN' WEST, TOO.

WEREN'T WE, FISK?

HUH?

UH...OH, YEAH. WE WERE JUST SAYIN'.

I MEAN, THEY'RE LOOKIN' FOR ALL THREE OF US. MIGHT AS WELL STICK TOGETHER, DON'T YOU THINK?

YEAH, YOU GUYS WON'T STICK OUT AT ALL ON THE ROAD.

THEN WE'LL STAY OFF THE ROAD.

BUT THREE HEADS ARE BETTER THAN ONE.

ESPECIALLY IF ONE OF THE HEADS IS MINE, WHICH IS AS GOOD AS THREE HEADS.

HERE WE GO.